Sandhurst Library
The Broadway
Sandhurst
GU47 9BL
01252 870161

D0831063

B/Sen 4/16

	28 APR 2017	4 JAN 2018	
13 NOV	09 JUN 17	23 JAN 2018	
12 NOV	26 JUN 17	13 APR 2018	
10 DEC	29 JUL 17		
09 FEB 17		05 MAY 2018	
	24 AUG 2017		
02 MAR 17	12 SEP 2017		
07 AUG 17			
	5 OCT 2017		

To avoid overdue charges this book should be returned on or before the last date stamped above. If not required by another reader it may be renewed in person, by telephone, post or on-line at www.bracknell-forest.gov.uk/libraries

Library & Information Service

S1.cdr

44139001400922

For Annie
~A.M.

For the Farmhouse Mice
~T.W.

LITTLE TIGER PRESS
An imprint of Magi Publications
1 The Coda Centre,
189 Munster Road, London SW6 6AW
www.littletigerpress.com
First published in Great Britain 2002
This edition published in 2005
Text copyright © Alan MacDonald 2002
Illustrations copyright © Tim Warnes 2002
Alan MacDonald and Tim Warnes
have asserted their rights to be identified
as the author and illustrator of this
work under the Copyright, Designs
and Patents Act, 1988.
Printed in China
All rights reserved
ISBN 978-1-84506-346-7
10 9 8 7 6 5 4 3 2

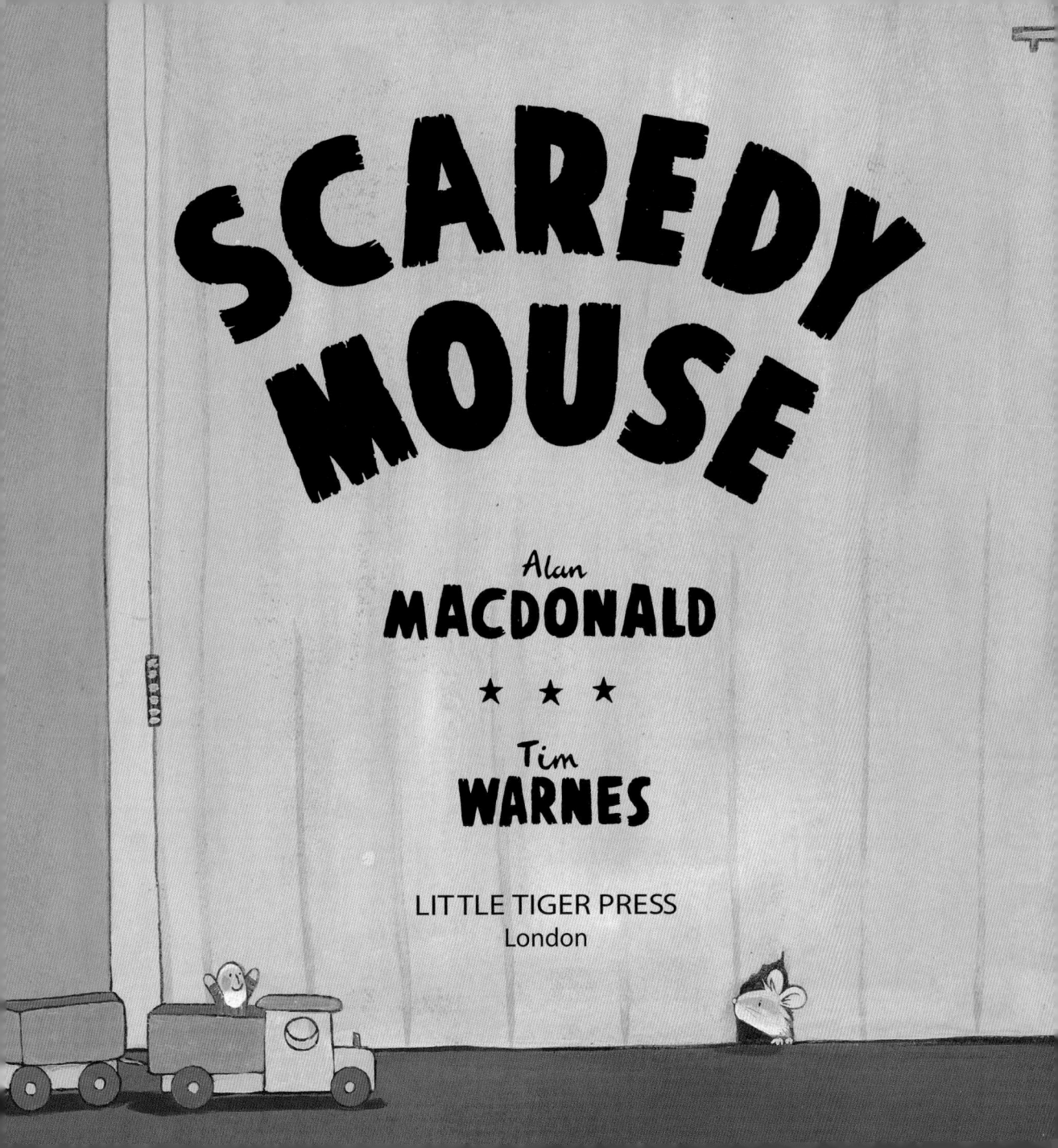
SCAREDY MOUSE
Alan
MACDONALD
★ ★ ★
Tim
WARNES
LITTLE TIGER PRESS
London

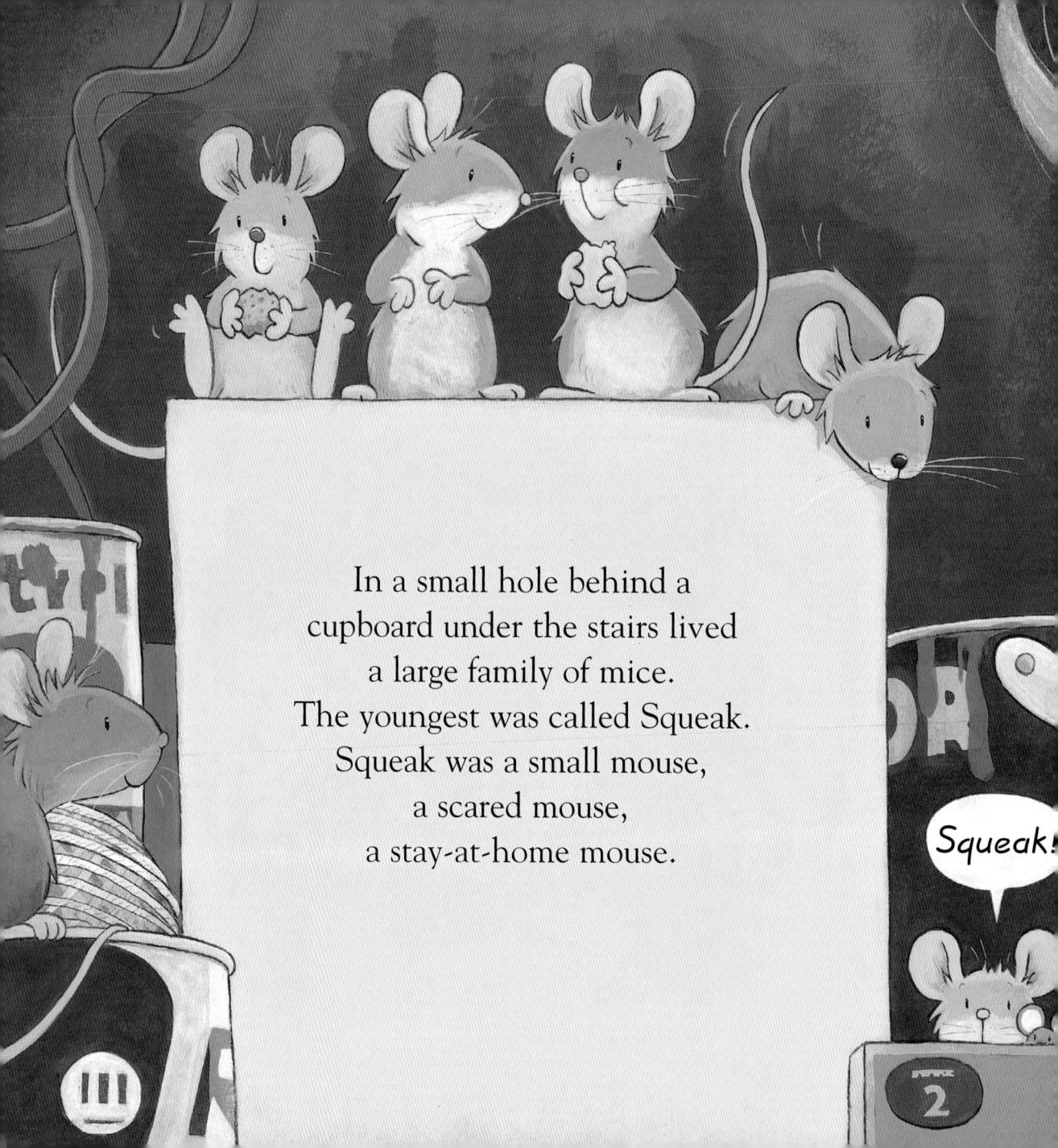

In a small hole behind a
cupboard under the stairs lived
a large family of mice.
The youngest was called Squeak.
Squeak was a small mouse,
a scared mouse,
a stay-at-home mouse.

One evening, Squeak was woken up
by his sister, Nibbles.
"Let's go to the kitchen," she said.
"I've just seen something yummy.
A chocolate cake as big as a wheel."

Squeak loved chocolate, but he was very scared.
"What if I get lost?" he worried. "What if we meet the big ginger cat with green eyes?"
"The ginger cat's asleep," said Nibbles. "And I know how to stop you getting lost."

Nibbles fetched a big ball of string, and tied one end round Squeak. "There," she said. "All you have to do is to follow the string and you'll find your way home."

They scurried out of the mousehole,
and into the dark, shadowy hall.
Squeak kept close to Nibbles, trailing
the string behind him. But as they crossed
the hall, Squeak saw a long, stripy tail.

"IT'S THE CAT, IT'S THE CAT!"
he cried.
Squeak ran this way and that,
harum-scarum, round and back.
"Don't be silly," said Nibbles . . .

Squeak slowly came out of his hiding place.

Through the dining room scampered Nibbles and Squeak. Under the table and under the chairs. But just as Squeak was about to eat a biscuit crumb, he saw two eyes gleaming in the dark.

"IT'S THE CAT, IT'S THE CAT!"
he cried.
Squeak ran this way and that,
harum-scarum, round and back.
"Don't be silly," said Nibbles . . .

Squeak smiled nervously.

Into the lounge they stole, past the fireplace, and past the ticking clock. Suddenly, Squeak froze in his tracks. There, peeping above the arm of the sofa, was a head with two sharp ears.

"IT'S THE CAT, IT'S THE CAT!"
he cried.
Squeak ran this way and that,
harum-scarum, round and back.
"Don't be silly," said Nibbles . . .

"Silly me!" said Squeak.

Into the kitchen tiptoed the two mice, across the floorboards and past the cupboard. Squeak peeped inside.
He shivered and shook.
There, in the shadows, was something furry.

"IT'S THE CAT,
IT'S THE CAT!"
he cried.
Squeak ran this way
and that, harum-scarum,
round and back.
"Don't be silly," said
Nibbles . . .

"Phew!" sighed Squeak.

Just then, Nibbles spotted the chocolate cake on the table. It didn't take them long to find their way up to it. Soon their paws and whiskers were licky and sticky with chocolate.

"Yum," sighed Nibbles. "I could eat all day."
Squeak was a hungry mouse,
but also a worried mouse,
a scared mouse,
a want-to-go-home mouse.

So Nibbles scrambled down the fridge . . .

and Squeak and the cake followed.

They heaved the cake across the floor, but . . .

just as they reached the door,
a shadow fell across their path.
"IT'S THE CAT, IT'S THE CAT!"
cried Squeak.
"Don't be silly," said Nibbles.
"It's only . . ."

THE CAT!
Run, Squeak!

Squeak ran this way and that,
harum-scarum, round and back.
The big ginger cat narrowed his eyes,
opened his claws and . . .

pounced.
But the cat found himself caught in a web of string. The more he struggled, the more he became tangled . . .

until soon he was tied up
like a fat ginger parcel.
A mad cat,
a sad cat,
a feeling-a-fool cat.

Squeak was no longer a small or a scared mouse.
He was a bold-as-a-lion mouse.

And the next time he met the
big ginger cat, he just said . . .

BOO!